SOFIA MARTINEZ

Singing Superstar

by Jacqueline Jules

illustrated by Kim Smith

PICTURE WINDOW BOOKS
a capstone imprint

Sofia Martinez is published by Picture Window Books,
A Capstone omprint
1710 Roe Crest Drive
North Mankato, Minnesota 56003
www.mycapstone.com

Library of Congress Cataloging-in-Publication Data
Jules, Jacqueline, 1956- author.
Singing superstar / by Jacqueline Jules ; illustrated by
Kim Smith.
pages cm. -- (Sofia Martinez)
Summary: Sofia's family does not want to hear her singing
anymore, so she must find the appropiate place to use her
new superstar-sing box machine.

ISBN 978-1-4795-8716-2 (library binding)
ISBN 978-1-4795-8722-3 (pbk.)
ISBN 978-1-4795-8726-1 (ebook pdf)

1. Singing--Juvenile fiction. 2. Hispanic American
children--Juvenile fiction. 3. Hispanic American
families--Juvenile fiction. [1. Singing--Fiction. 2.
Hispanic Americans--Fiction. 3. Family life--Fiction.]
I. Smith, Kim, 1986- illustrator. II. Title. III. Series:
Jules, Jacqueline, 1956- Sofia Martinez.

PZ7.J92947Si 2016
[E]--dc23   2015024982

Designer: Kay Fraser

Printed in the United States of America in
North Mankato, Minnesota.
062017 010578R

TABLE OF CONTENTS

CHAPTER 1

The Best Gift

It was Christmas! Sofia and her family headed to her abuela's house to open gifts. Sofia's cousin Hector and his family came, too.

Mamá and Papá gave Sofia a board game. It looked fun, but it was not what Sofia was hoping for.

Her sisters, Elena and Luisa,

gave Sofia a pink sweater.

"¡Bonito!" Sofia said. "¡Gracias!"

It still wasn't the present Sofia

was dreaming of.

Abuela handed a box to Sofia.

"Here you go, my sweet Sofia."

Sofia tore off the wrapping
paper and squealed with joy.

"A Superstar Sing Box!" she
yelled.

Sofia picked up the microphone and sang while the rest of her family opened presents.

"¡Feliz Navidad! ¡Feliz Navidad!"

Sofia sang the song five times in a row. She was ready to sing it again when Mamá interrupted.

"No más música, Sofia. Sit down for Christmas dinner," she said.

After dessert, Sofia picked up her microphone again.

Elena and Luisa groaned. Baby
Mariela put her hands over her
ears and cried.

Tía Carmen grabbed Mariela.
Tío Miguel rushed to get their
coats. Hector and his brothers
were leaving, too!

"Don't go!" Sofia cried. "I want to sing for you. You can even sing *with* me if you want."

"Maybe tomorrow." Hector said as he waved. "¡Hasta luego!"

CHAPTER 2

Nonstop Singing

Early the next morning, Sofia tiptoed downstairs with her singing machine.

She climbed onto the coffee table, using it as a stage. Sofia swayed and spun, pretending her nightgown was a fancy dress.

Sofia loved the sound of her voice through the microphone.

Mamá called down the stairs. "¡No más música! The family is trying to sleep."

Sofia waited for Mamá and Papá to come down for breakfast. She had the microphone ready when they walked into the kitchen.

"¡Feliz Navidad! ¡Feliz Navidad!" Sofia sang loudly.

Papá rubbed his head. "That's the same song you sang last night."

"Yo sé," Sofia said. "It's my best one!"

"You know lots of songs," Mamá said. "What about Los Pollitos or De Colores?"

"Sometimes I forget the words," Sofia said.

"We can fix that," Mamá said.

"Come with me to the piano."

Mamá and Sofia practiced until Sofia knew all the words.

"Gracias, Mamá. I'll go sing for Papá," Sofia said.

Papá was in the basement watching soccer. Sofia had to turn the volume up on her machine so Papá could hear her over the soccer match.

"Do you like my singing?" Sofia asked loudly.

"Sí," Papá said, his eyes on the screen. "The rest of the family should hear you, too. Go visit your cousin Hector."

"Good idea!" Sofia said.

CHAPTER 3

A Place for a Star

Sofia carried her singing machine across the yard to her cousins' house. But as soon as she started singing, Tía Carmen stopped her.

"Ahora no, Sofia," she said. "Baby Mariela is taking her nap."

"You could sing outside," Hector said.

"Hace frío," Sofia said. "And I
don't have my hat."

"It's not that cold out, and you
can borrow one from my Mamá."

Hector took a fluffy hat and
leather gloves out of the closet.

"¡Elegante!" Sofia said. "With these on, I feel like a star."

"You look like one, too," Hector said.

Hector and Sofia went outside and stood on the corner with the Superstar Sing Box.

"I'll give a concert for the neighborhood," Sofia said.

One of the neighbors walked by with a dog. The dog sat down to sing with Sofia. "AROOO!"

Soon, another neighbor came by with a dog. "AROOO!"

"Sofia!" Hector shouted. "The dogs love you!"

Sofia had fun singing until a third dog came by. This one was bigger and had a very loud bark.

"ARF! ARF! ARF!"

Sofia couldn't hear her own voice anymore.

"¡Silencio!" she told the big dog.

But he was too excited to listen.

"ARF! ARF! ARF!"

Sofia frowned.

"I'm going inside!" she told

Hector. "I'll sing for my sisters."

But Elena and Luisa were tired

of listening to Sofia.

"Go see **Abuela**," Luisa said.

"She gave you the machine."

"¡Claro!" Sofia said.

A little while later, Sofia was at her abuela's house. She set up her machine. Then she turned the volume up and loudly sang. Sofia smiled and swayed like she was on TV.

Abuela clapped. "¡Maravilloso! Sing it again!"

Finally, Sofia had found the perfect audience!

Talk It Out

1. Sofia loves her family. Talk about your family and what you love about them.

2. Why did people keep telling Sofia to sing somewhere else? How do you think this made her feel?

3. If you had to pick just one song to sing, what would it be and why?

Write It Down

1. Pretend you are Sofia. Write a journal entry about your new singing machine.

2. Sofia loved her new singing machine. Write about the best gift you've ever received.

3. Write a paragraph describing Sofia's singing from one of the dog's point of view.

About the Author

Jacqueline Jules is the award-winning author of numerous children's books, including *No English* (2012 Forward National Literature Award), *Zapato Power: Freddie Ramos Takes Off* (2010 CYBILS Literary Award, Maryland Blue Crab Young Reader Honor Award, and ALSC Great Early Elementary Reads), and *Freddie Ramos Makes a Splash* (named on 2013 List of Best Children's Books of the Year by Bank Street College Committee).

When not reading, writing, or teaching, Jacqueline enjoys time with her family in northern Virginia.

About the Illustrator

Kim Smith has worked in magazines, advertising, animation, and children's gaming. She studied illustration at the Alberta College of Art and Design in Calgary, Alberta, where she now resides.

Kim is the illustrator of the middle-grade mystery series *The Ghost and Max Monroe*, the picture book *Over the River and Through the Woods*, and the cover of the middle-grade novel *How to Make a Million*.

FUN
doesn't stop here!

- Videos & Contests
- Games & Puzzles
- Friends & Favorites
- Authors & Illustrators

Discover more at
www.capstonekids.com

See you soon!
¡Nos Vemos pronto!